THE FIFTIES AND SIXTIES

LUNCH BOX

THE FIFTIES AND SIXTIES

LUNCH BOX

SCOTT BRUCE

PRINCIPAL PHOTOGRAPHY BY DAN SOPER

CHRONICLE BOOKS • SAN FRANCISCO

Dedication

To Beverly, for love and support and for insisting on lunch box free zones
throughout the apartment

Edited by Judith Dunham
Book and cover design by Seventeenth Street Studios
Typesetting by Another Point

Printed in Japan

Library of Congress Cataloging-in-Publication Data

Bruce, Scott.
  Lunch box.

    1. Lunchboxes—United States—Collectors and collecting—United States. I. Soper,
Dan. II. Title.
NK6213.B7   1988   683'.8   88-18959
ISBN 0-87701-535-X

Distributed in Canada by Raincoast Books   112 East Third Avenue   Vancouver, British
Columbia V5T 1C8
10 9 8 7 6 5 4 3 2 1

Chronicle Books
275 5th Street
San Francisco, California 94103

WHAT'S FOR LUNCH

Hopalong Cassidy, Aladdin Industries, 1950–53.
The granddaddy of them all. "Overnight," says Aladdin, "the mundane, boring
lunch box trade became Big Business."

INTRODUCTION

*Popular, transient, expendable, low cost, mass-pro-
duced, young, witty, sexy, gimmicky, glamorous, and
last, but not least, Big Business.*
    RICHARD HAMILTON'S DEFINITION OF POPULAR CULTURE

A LUNCH BOX ADVERTISEMENT BLURTED "Nothing like it has ever been seen before in the annals of entertainment," and it was right. Between 1950 and 1970 over 120 million lunch boxes were sold in America—one and one-half boxes for every boy and girl of the baby boom era. For our generation, striking out to school through the forbidding landscape of a subdivision just gouged from a forest or truck farm, through muddy streets littered with giant earth-moving equipment and gaping concrete sewer pipes, a provisioned lunch box was equipment as essential as a rifle had been to earlier pioneers—a shield against an uncertain future, a badge of membership, a friend. If the icon of the age, the star of the *Leave it to Beaver* show, carried a plain box, we understood, because his picturesque neighborhood, tame by our raw standards, didn't call out for the robust protection of a *Davy Crockett* or *Tom Corbett* box.

In addition to the postwar affluence that enabled decorated kits to fit the family budget as well as a brown paper bag, the key to the spectacular box boom was the television. The newly invented appliance was in millions of homes by the early fifties. The friendly cast of the TV became a reassuring electronic anchor in every topsy-turvy suburban homestead. For kids born into this life, TV offered compelling frontier fantasies that resonated with the new life-style. Through this culture of consumption, baby boomers across far-flung suburbs crystallized into an informal electronic tribe.

Lunch boxes emblazoned with vibrant icons of favorite video chiefs quickly became symbolic affirmations of their young owners, much as finned cars were for their parents. The ostentatious highway for boxes was, of course, the road to school. Leaving the house at 8:30 every weekday, boxes blew our horns. In the blackboard jungle, the lunch box, reflecting one's identification with a fashionable character or show, was a passport to either social acceptance or, as in the case of *Red Plaid*, oblivion.

Recognizing TV as a threat to its authority, the educational system early on circled its wagons against the media. Condemned to the school "reservation," our tribe saw lunch boxes as Trojan horses, whisking TV in through the side door of the place where it was barred from the front. The big set in the classroom corner may have been

Peanut butter and jelly, the bedrock of a boomer's lunch.

on only a half hour a day during foreign language class, but those thirty small sets on the coatrack shelf never stopped broadcasting. When the lunch bell rang, the wooden horses' trapdoors sprang open and out into the cafeteria poured the video pantheon. With every bite of sandwich and sip of soup, reruns of last night's episode blew tumbleweeds and rocket exhaust around the linoleum. Predictably, most private schools saw boxes as reservation rum and outlawed them.

Ironically, it wasn't the PTA, but the example of Davy Crockett swinging his rifle at the Alamo that doomed the classic steel box. Ralph Nader's 1962 book, *Unsafe at Any Speed,* had attacked GM's Corvair car as a deathtrap and launched a critical look at the safety of American industrial products. By the early seventies, a gaggle of militant

mothers (probably those who forced *Red Plaid* on their sons) insisted that the steel box was a killer, a classroom Corvair. After they paraded alleged victims of box "brain bashing" past the Florida legislature, a ban was slapped on the sale of steel boxes. Other legislatures soon fell to the inquisition.

As markets for the steel lunch box shrank state by state, steel was phased out in favor of the universally welcomed, "safe" plastic boxes. The change marked the end of an era. Lunch box manufacturers, called "boxmen," wept into their hands.

BOX DESIGN HISTORY

Like every legend, *Hoppy,* the first TV character lunch box, has a log cabin story. In the spring of 1949, a few executives at Aladdin industries, a vacuum bottle maker, were sitting at a conference table and tossing around ideas to increase slumping sales.

"Why don't we put decals on the faces of these plain red and blue lunch boxes we've been selling," asked one, "like cowboys and Indians?"

"Not just cowboys and Indians," said another. "How about putting on a TV character decal—like *Hopalong Cassidy*?"

A timely idea. To design the *Hopalong Cassidy* kit, Aladdin hired Chicago industrial designer Robert O. Burton, who in two years would create another icon of American culture—the red and white striped Kentucky Fried Chicken logo. "*Hoppy* was born around the dining room table at one in the morning," says a boxman who was there. "After clearing away the dirty dishes, Burton made the first rough chalk drawing. We pasted it on a plain red box and in a couple of days walked away with a big advance order of fifty thousand. We got a $10,000 guarantee and five percent royalties."

The reaction to *Hoppy* in the fall of 1950 was far greater than boxmen expected. "We recognized," recounts Aladdin, "that if you could develop kits with favorite TV characters, you'd create a bonanza! Overnight, the mundane, boring lunch box trade became Big Business. . . . We sold a staggering six hundred thousand *Hoppy* kits the first year."

"True," admitted Aladdin, "*Hoppy* wasn't the very first character lunch box." A few prophetic stabs resembling pressed ham cans had been produced by other manufacturers from the turn of the century through the Depression. But small and expensive, bottleless, and "without the continuous promotion of TV," the glorified tobacco tins merely played John the Baptist to *Hoppy*'s Messiah.

So for kids waking up from the scarcity of goods imposed by years under a strict war economy, Aladdin's *Hoppy* box, with its four-inch decal the size of existing TV screens, was a revelation. Aladdin had even greater success with its 1952 *Tom Corbett, Space Cadet* kit, also made with a decal. A handle was put on the final frontier, and sales thundered into orbit.

THE FULLY LITHOGRAPHED BOX
Jealous of his TV rival's success, Roy Rogers wanted his own lunch box. Rebuffed by Aladdin—"One cowboy is enough"—he rode

Roy Rogers catalog page, American Thermos, 1953.
A breakthrough over *Hoppy*'s decal, American Thermos's fully lithographed TV screen sold 2½ million boxes and immediately became the industry standard.

north to American Thermos, a Connecticut vacuum bottle maker (after 1959 called King Seeley Thermos or KST). Having watched Aladdin's success, American Thermos was intrigued but hesitated, fearing character boxes might be just a fad. Finally, on Roy's third try, they swallowed the idea.

Trotted out in 1953, the *Roy Rogers & Dale Evans* lunch box, with its big full-picture screen, surrounded, like a high-priced console, on all sides by blond wood grain, perfected the TV set metaphor. Fully lithographed steel, accomplished by a technique similar to that used to create the popular tin litho garages then on the market, it was an even bigger smash than *Hoppy*. The first year, 2½ million kits sold, increasing Thermos's overall sales by twenty percent.

Box Macho

Like the fascination with the big finned cars of the fifties, the appeal of lunch boxes was emotional. Between birth and the brown bag, you weren't what you *drove* but what you *carried*. Your net worth in the blackboard jungle was broadcast by that box dangling from your fingers.

The shiny showrooms for lunch boxes were supermarket aisles. The two box choices of 1952 had exploded, by the end of the decade, to a dozen or more options from each competing manufacturer, promising that the box picked—though stamped out on an assembly line—reflected the *real you*.

It's not surprising, then, that the shelf above the coatrack read like a parking lot. A blue *Beatles* flashed "hip"; the class princess carried a sleek *Barbie;* her nemesis, the class clown, carried *Get Smart;* the beleaguered new guy had the *Chuck Wagon*, with scenes of staving off an attack; that firecracker-throwing, crazy kid bashed around a *Buccaneer;* and, naturally, everyone felt superior to that poor kid whose mom made him carry a *Red Plaid*.

With so much at stake, getting the *right* box every fall was a big deal. At $2.39 for a 1950 *Hopalong Cassidy* kit and up to $3.50 for a 1969 *Laugh-In*, you needed mom's deep pocket. No wonder that, with all the skirt tugging, store personnel came to call the box display the "whine sign."

Knocked down but not out, Aladdin bit back. "The *Roy Rogers* character wasn't as popular as our *Hoppy* kit," sniffed Aladdin, "but it was OK." Dumping their upstaged, baked enamel boxes, Aladdin retooled, adopting American Thermos's full-picture lithographed innovation for the very successful 1954 line.

So did a couple of newcomers to the business. Smelling profitable inroads into a mass of young consumers, two other metal stamping outfits, ADCO Liberty and Universal (Landers, Frary & Clark), entered the lunch box market in 1954. Ohio Art, better known as the maker of Etch-A-Sketch, had made basket-type lunch pails since the thirties, but didn't switch over to the new industry standard until 1957.

By the midfifties, competition between box makers was getting stiff. To keep its edge, Aladdin had Robert O. Burton improve the band, that equatorial region around the middle of the box. Knowing that, as on any frontier, violence was the answer, Burton invented two very popular solutions. Beginning in 1956, he wrapped Western boxes with very convincing tooled leather gun belts and introduced the panoramic band—a series of interlocking scenes, often of battle.

In 1962, Burton's protégé, Elmer Lehnhardt, introduced "3-D" embossing to the flat box. Lehnhardt had been a TV wrestler, and the experience apparently left him frustrated by the flatness of action characters on the boxes' surfaces. At his urging, Aladdin engineers altered the metal stamping dies to elevate key figures in relief to give them more dimension. This braille effect became an Aladdin trademark.

In the late sixties, KST briefly experimented with spin games on the back of nonlicensed boxes. Designed by artist Nick LoBianco, the games used fly-sized magnetic playing pieces, but were dropped when kids showed little interest.

DOMES

The apex of box design was, arguably, the decorated dome. Lithographed versions of the familiar workman's lunch box, these boxes, often generics, were created "to take up the slack between idols and to cut down on development costs," says Aladdin. Burton's first dome, *Buccaneer* of 1957, capitalizing on a national pirate craze, was a brilliant success.

Like the TV set boxes that opened windows onto the media landscape, domes advanced any fantasy of travel or conquest that could be made to conform to the basic dome shape, as the witty succession of buildings, locomotives, covered wagons, and cable cars illustrated. After *Buccaneer,* both Aladdin and KST had at least one dome in their yearly lineup.

VINYLS

The idea of a vinyl lunch box came from outside the box industry. Looking for new worlds to conquer, Standard Plastic Products, a New Jersey manufacturer with a fast-selling line of *Ponytail* vinyl school accessories, approached KST about a box in 1958. "It was the logical next step," says KST. "We bought the idea." An array of vinyl boxes, in pastels for girls and earth tones for boys, hit the stores in 1959.

Aladdin caught wind of KST's coup and, unwilling "to let anyone get the edge," rushed their vinyl contender, *Bobby Soxer,* into production in time for the midseason.

Boxmen never were very comfortable with vinyls: They were a "pretty bad kit. Just a piece of shower curtain plastic, heat sealed over cardboard," says KST. "You'd get it out in the rain, and that was about it. . . . Who knows what kind of stuff would *grow* in there!" If that wasn't enough, "the decoration was *stinko,*" groused KST. Although vinyl sales reached thirty percent of the total market in the sixties, thanks largely to KST's *Barbie* line, comparatively few boomer vinyls have survived into the present.

Wishing to hang on to their petite customers after they'd outgrown their first boxes, Aladdin added purselike vinyl boxes with long handles, called Brunch Bags, in 1962. Targeted mainly at preteens in the third- to sixth-grade range, boxmen did well by this "sophisticated" upgrade option. Brunch Bags such as *The Beatles* and *The Flying Nun* were licensed, but most were embellished with dull, generic patterns.

BITING THE DUST

Like their automobile counterparts, Nash and Studebaker, ADCO and Universal couldn't put a dent into the market share of the box industry leaders. ADCO dropped out of box production in 1956 after making the blunder of putting a non-Disney character on the back of an "official" box. Universal was bought by General Electric in 1963, which closed down the entire box and vacuum bottle operation. "Not much of a risk taker," in its own words, Ohio Art quit the business in 1985. "The little guys bit the dust," says KST, "because they were

VW Bus, Omni Graphics, 1960s.
Domes offered further choices for self-expression.

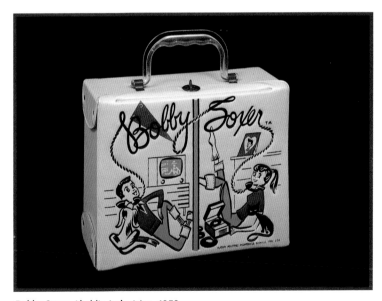

Bobby Soxer, Aladdin Industries, 1959.
Vinyl boxes were introduced in 1959 to satisfy noisy critics.

In the tradition of southern television ministries, Aladdin's anchorman takes box fever to the world in 1952. Their new headquarters, built with *Hoppy* kit profits, shines in the background.

Electronic Landscape

Impervious to blackouts and vertical rolling, but not rust, the TV screen format of lunch boxes captured the baby boomers' electronic landscape. From *Tom Corbett* running breathlessly back to the main set from the wings after pitching a live Ovaltine commercial to the dramatic moon walk where each breath threatened to be the astronaut's last, over one hundred boomer TV series, special events, and commercials were boxed.

Boxes were fine-tuned to TV. Aladdin's first *Hopalong Cassidy* had a four-inch decal no bigger than the TV screen of the late forties. The "improved reception" of American Thermos's 1953 full-screen *Roy Rogers* box paralleled the jump to bigger, ten-inch TV screens the year before. Boxes such as *Land of the Giants* are brilliant because they transmit the excitement of what TV conveys best—looming, planetary heads.

Just such a head on TV was LBJ, who anticipated the boxing experience with his habit of watching programming on the three networks at once. Set out the *Cowboy in Africa, Gunsmoke,* and *The Monkees* boxes, and we see what he watched at 7:30 on a Monday night in 1967—burdened by Vietnam *and* that beagle in his lap. Set out a dozen cartoon boxes, and the *Hot Wheels, Kellogg's Breakfast,* and *Barbie* boxes, and you've got what the president woke up to on a typical Saturday morning.

Every TV box marked a contested and inevitably lost national ratings spot. A few popular shows, such as *Gunsmoke,* sprawled across a decade and produced several different versions—in the case of *Bonanza,* one for every time a Cartwright left the Ponderosa. Obscure series, like *Space Explorer,* burned up in the airwaves months before the box hit the stores and left boxmen buried under the dead stock and "sickened on space."

bucking the two bigger names of Aladdin and us—a goddamn vise. We'd come into the trade shows where the important buyers were with impressive store displays and free promo kits. Who wouldn't go for the better package?"

By the early seventies, even the vise was up against the wall. As a cost-cutting measure, Aladdin had gone over to plastic bottles in 1968, and KST had followed in 1972. But the ban on the sale of the steel box was closing down markets, so Aladdin and KST began the gradual phaseout of steel boxes in favor of injection-molded plastic. By 1987, all steel box production by the major manufacturers had ceased.

MEET THE ARTISTS

Reflecting the tremendous innovation and energy of the boom, the lion's share of boxes of the fifties and sixties were created by four commercial artists. Split between Aladdin and KST, these men had characters as colorful as the boxes they lovingly created. Although they were not household names, many of their other artistic accomplishments are still the peanut butter and jelly of the contemporary world. Let's meet them.

ROBERT O. BURTON

Anyone who has had their eyes knocked out by the inside of a Big Boy or an Elby coffee shop, or has seen the red and white striped Kentucky Fried Chicken logo, has entered the imagination of industrial designer Robert O. Burton. But none of his brainchildren from the fifties are as well-loved as his lunch boxes.

Like Big Boy in his checkered pants bringing burgers to the world, Burton fathered most of Aladdin's boxes in the fifties, including the original *Hoppy.* Referred to as "one hell of a guy" inside the company, he is often remembered for his pranks. Following Michelangelo's example in the Sistine Chapel, he painted himself as a floating cadet on the 1954 *Tom Corbett* box. When discovered—"you're not getting away with this"—he capitulated, but a couple of years later coyly placed his sovereign profile on a couple of ten reales coins on the *Buccaneer* dome, his masterpiece. (page 104).

That beautiful muzzle-flash orange and emerald green box, with

Designer of the Kentucky Fried Chicken logo, Big Boy coffee shop decor, and Aladdin's boxes in the fifties, industrial designer Robert O. Burton created his masterpiece, *Buccaneer,* to resemble one of his swank restaurant interiors turned inside out.

its looted coins filling the vault and a mean shark patrolling Davy Jones's locker on the bottom, smacks of one of his firecracker restaurant interiors turned inside out. Every detail advances the overall design.

About the time of *Sputnik,* Burton was begged by the helpless citizenry of Chicago to design a new lighting system for their famous State Street shopping mecca. Providing a break from sketching the *Zorro* box, his futuristic lamp poles apparently looked enough like golf clubs that President Eisenhower threw the switch from the White House via the *Vanguard* satellite for the opening ceremony.

ELMER LEHNHARDT

One of TV's first wrestlers in Chicago's Marigold Ballroom, Elmer Lehnhardt turned to commercial art in 1949 under the brush of Haddon Sundbloom, creator of the Coca-Cola Santa Claus, who recognized Lehnhardt's gift for drawing likenesses. Recruited early by Burton to finish kit artwork at Aladdin, Lehnhardt rose to art director in the sixties when he worked hard to bring KST to the mat. He

License to Pail

"They hated our *guts* and we hated *theirs,*" confides KST about its rival lunch box manufacturer, Aladdin. Like Coke and Pepsi, Nashville's Aladdin and Connecticut's KST were locked in a fight where millions of dollars were in the balance.

Keeping the edge depended on "getting the hot properties, the licensed characters from TV," says Aladdin, and in the fifties, "getting those properties, at $10,000 down and five percent royalties, was a lot of fun because the TV networks controlled the shows and they'd rent a New York City hotel floor and preview them all. We'd try to sew up the first refusal rights on as many prime-time properties as we could."

Almost. "We made mistakes," admits Aladdin, "like *Barbie* or *Peanuts,* which was offered to us in the sixties but at the time it seemed *too* adult. We thought *Hogan's Heroes* was a better bet, so we passed on *Peanuts.* It turned out to be a windfall for the *competition.*"

"Damn right because *we* were the industry leader," snarls KST, "*except* when we passed up *Batman.* The *competition* got it and, well . . . it was a big winner."

Without figures to settle the score, cooler heads agree, "It was a two-horse race with a lot of give and take. A strong property would be the bellwether of the season and the biggest market share. Sometimes *they* had it, sometimes *we* did."

Boxmen staked out supermarket aisles to see who actually bought their product. "We *agonized* over who made the decision. First the kid runs over to pick out favorites from the display and then the mother comes along," says Aladdin. "Most of the time they only agreed over *Disney*"—or "*Peanuts,*" adds KST.

Like the gumshoe on this 1967 store display, boxmen staked out supermarket aisles to see who really bought their kits.

The Creative Process

Kit charisma hinged on character recognition, like Flipper's smirk or Howdy's gapped-tooth grin. Always pressed for time, box artists had to capture that elusive star quality on the fly. Robert Burton worked at home in front of his family's nineteen-inch GE set, and Nick LoBianco, on the way to his Manhattan studio, leafed through *Time* or *TV Guide* for glimpses of upcoming shows.

"Most of the time we worked totally blind," says LoBianco. "If the TV show or movie was still in the early production stages, I'd get a private screening. For *Get Smart,* the studio took me over and showed me the rough cut, then gave me a few 8 by 10 glossies of Don Adams and Barbara Feldon and that was it. I had to design the box from memory from a single ten-minute screening." John Henry, creator of the *007* box, says, "Sometimes it took all the talent I had just to get an image to fit around the band."

Often the obstacles breathed. Unflattered by the brushwork of his face, English actor Rex Harrison drove Elmer Lehnhardt "just about nuts" by rejecting his *Dr. Dolittle* art five times. "Yup," nods LoBianco, told of Lehnhardt's trial, "Diahann Carroll was a bitch about her *Julia* box too."

For all their pains, free-lance artists earned $500 to $700 per kit in the sixties. Where is their original artwork (usually temperas twice actual size) today? None of Thermos's, ADCO's, and Universal's survives, but most of Aladdin's, including *The Beatles* and *Star Trek,* slumber under lock and key in the company's archives.

Artist Elmer Lehnhardt found actor Rex Harrison as impossible to box as the two-headed Push-Me-Pull-You in *Dr. Dolittle.*

TV-wrestler-turned-box-artist, Aladdin's Elmer Lehnhardt poses as Matt Dillon for a *Gunsmoke* box composition. During the sixties, he fought hard to bring KST to the mat.

somehow found the time to demonstrate the tricks of his past profession during office coffee breaks.

Lehnhardt's wrestler's imagination, manifested in a sense of surprise movement and mass, was brought into the ring of each box composition. His itch for more to grab on to was behind Aladdin's decision to emboss their flat boxes in 1962. An amateur photographer and a ham, as evidenced by his demonic self-portrait on the *Land of the Giants* box, he often pictured himself in action poses, such as with Marshal Matt Dillon, to incorporate into box art.

But like the shadow cast by his cowboy hat, the artist had his dark side. Before his death in 1985, Lehnhardt, whose anonymously created boxes were enjoyed by millions, was jealous of the recognition lavished on nonrealistic modernists such as Picasso and Matisse.

ED WEXLER

If the hydroplane driver's red helmet on the *Boating* box shines like a succulent maraschino cherry, the airplane fuselages on *Hometown Airport* resemble red peppers, or, at a glance, the golden palomino on the *Trigger* box looks like a rearing Cornish game hen, you're not going crazy. The artist, Ed Wexler, specialized in illustrating food labels for American Can, the company that manufactured all of American Thermos's steel boxes until 1964.

Wexler, who despite his obsession "wasn't stout," according to a fellow canman, "had a flair for making the label roll around in your mouth. If a package had to look *really tempting and delicious,* we threw it to Ed." Between hundreds of labels for Puss 'n Boots, Stokely's Finest, and Spam, Wexler created most of Thermos's kit art through 1961. As if fighting a fear that he was just another artist on the shelf, he often snaked his signature through the prairie grass on a box's picture.

Roy Rogers and Dale Evans loved Wexler's mouth-watering artwork, in part because the kits were the biggest-selling merchandise made for their show. Rumor has it that the appreciative cowboy sang "Happy Trails" over the phone on Wexler's retirement from American Can in 1964.

NICK LOBIANCO

What do all the zillions of merchandising incarnations of *Snoopy* and his brat pack, *The Monkees* guitar logo, and the fabulous *Lost In Space* lunch box have in common? All are the work of Nick LoBianco, an imperial free-lancer, who from his New York City studio dominated KST's box art from 1962 until the midseventies.

An artistic whiz kid, LoBianco got his first commercial art job at sixteen and painted his first lunch box, *Beany & Cecil,* at twenty-two. Except in his dome masterpiece, *Lost In Space,* LoBianco pitted his flat-shaped figures against static backgrounds of solid, usually rectangular color—an effect that resembles a cartoon cell. "The reasons were both artistic and technical," LoBianco says. "Sure, I picked up tricks along the way, but the bumped-up patches of primary color had more to do with the limitations of lithography." LoBianco was comfortable forging cartoon styles, and it was his 1966 *Peanuts* box that persuaded Charles Schulz to throw LoBianco worldwide *Peanuts* merchandising rights, meaning that every *Peanuts* character you see, except the syndicated comic strip, actually comes from LoBianco's pen.

When crushed for time, LoBianco hired friends to finish box art, including two legendary artists from EC Comics and *MAD* magazine, Wally Wood and Jack Davis.

Yes, the hydroplane driver's helmet does look like a maraschino cherry. Food illustrator Ed Wexler painted most of American Thermos's boxes in the fifties, including the mouth-watering 1959–61 *Boating.*

Nick LoBianco, the prolific ghost artist for Charles Schulz's *Peanuts* merchandise, created The Monkees logo and most of KST's boxes in the sixties from his New York studio.

Roy Rogers, American Thermos, 1957–59.
Roy, Dale, and hot dog Russell visit on this jewel by Ed Wexler.

CHUCK WAGONS

A TRAIL BOX, IN THE hands of an imaginative kid, was the next best thing to a silver bullet. It turned the chalk-dust-covered floor into high desert strewn with prickly pear; buzzards circled in the acoustical tiling; desks stampeded like cattle; and the trip to the bathroom was fraught with diamondback rattlers and coyote. Maybe, on returning to the classroom, after pausing for a drink at the hallway spring, the teacher would be wearing a saddle and reins. *Giddyap!*

First to patent this magic with *Hoppy*, Aladdin boasts that "by the late fifties, we had every cowboy known."

Nearly. Of the horse opera stars, ADCO Liberty corralled *The Lone Ranger*, Universal roped *Gene Autry*, and American Thermos, of course, stabled the prolific *Roy Rogers & Dale Evans* after Aladdin, incredibly, turned the singing cowboy down. Roy Rogers's dynasty of twelve kits holds a single series record, although few of those boxes are exceptional.

Still, Aladdin's grip on the Western was undeniable, thanks first to the innovative treatment of the waist of the box, called the band. In 1956, Burton equipped the band of several boxes with hip-hugging, tooled leather gun belts. They looked so real that they gave crosswalk cops pause.

After a shaky start in 1959—when five thousand *Gunsmoke* boxes were distributed to prospective wholesale buyers before a secretary noticed that the Marshal in Marshal Matt Dillon had been spelled with an extra *L*—Aladdin nailed down the so-called adult Westerns of the sixties. Instrumental to the conquest was exwrestler Elmer Lehnhardt, who in 1962 brought the action further to life by embossing figures on the box faces. Few licensed properties from this period slipped through the fence into KST's spread.

Later in the decade, as the country woke up to the fact that Vietnam wasn't the OK Corral, the sun set on the Western, for all the trouble its implied values caused. Without missing a beat, TV producers kept audiences tuned in by splicing in other genres, like *James Bond* and *Tarzan,* and created bizarre recombinant Westerns, such as *Wild, Wild West* and *Cowboy in Africa*. As Nick LoBianco's *Cowboy in Africa* kit illustrates, KST excelled in boxing this exotica.

Gene Autry, Universal, 1954–55.

The Lone Ranger, ADCO Liberty, 1955.

Annie Oakley, Aladdin Industries, 1956.
Spinning off from *Gene Autry,* straight-shooting Annie became the first cowgirl to

Brave Eagle, American Thermos, 1956.
The Cheyenne chief charges his rival on Ed Wexler's box for the

Trigger, American Thermos, 1956.
Ed Wexler's golden palomino looks like a rearing Cornish game hen, which may
explain why Roy later had Trigger stuffed.

Roy Rogers Chow Wagon, American Thermos, 1958–61.
After driving a record nine box models down the decade, Roy and Dale take a
well-deserved break.

Paladin, Aladdin Industries, 1960.
A strong box by Bob Burton featuring *Paladin* (Richard Boone), named for his
chess knight calling card.

Pioneered by Bob Burton, Western box bands simulated tooled leather
gun holsters.

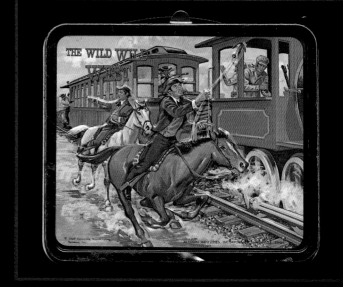

The look of Elmer Lehnhardt's West. Aladdin's exwrestler artist painted these four boxes for TV series of the sixties: (top left) *Gunsmoke*, 1959–61; (top right) *The Monroes*, 1967; (bottom left) *The Rifleman*, 1961–62; (bottom right) *Wild, Wild West*, 1969.

Bonanza, Aladdin Industries, 1968–69.
Lehnhardt captured the Cartwrights, Ben, Hoss, and Little Joe, defending the
Ponderosa. One of three boxes made for the show.

The look of Nick LoBianco's West: *Wagon Train,* 1964–65, and *The Guns of Will Sonnett,* 1968. A New Yorker who rarely ventured outside the city, KST's hired gun gave Western kits a vibrancy suggesting that peyote brew, not whiskey, was cactus country's preferred drink.

Cowboy in Africa production sheet and kit, King Seeley Thermos, 1968. "I had no idea what the series was about," said LoBianco about creating the king of the recombinant Western kits, "except what Lucas Mc . . . *ah* . . . Chuck Connors looked like. I remember researching those African animals and wondering about the lurid colors, then *bang* . . . it came together . . . God, I wish I still had that piece."

Howdy Doody, ADCO Liberty, 1954.
This landmark box was yanked from the market after Princess SummerFall
WinterSpring (Judy Tyler) defected to star opposite Elvis in *Jailhouse Rock*.

TIN KID VID

HOWDY DOODY MAY HAVE LAUNCHED ten thousand TV sets, but his Princess SummerFall WinterSpring launched the gapped-toothed guru's lunch box. Before she ditched Howdy for Elvis Presley, the sexy Indian maiden, played by Judy Tyler, was America's sweetheart. Says Howdy box artist Milt Neil, who also created the Phineas T. Bluster, Dilly Dally, and Flub-a-Dub characters, "She was tremendously popular. Sixty million kids watched her every day, so I put her on the kit."

The box was one of Doodyville's greatest hits. "Kids in the Peanut Gallery used to hold up their boxes and say 'Hey, we got the lunch box,'" says Neil, "which immediately earned them a squirt from Clarabell. We even gave away a few on the show as prizes." Neil is still uneasy with part of his baby: "The history lesson on the box's back wasn't my idea. It was decided way up in the company to satisfy Howdy's critics that the show had content."

Critics may have been right, but real trouble started when Howdy's rival, the King, wanted Judy Tyler as *his* princess. After she stunned Doodyville by defecting to play opposite Elvis Presley in *Jailhouse Rock*, "we yanked the box," says Neil, moodily, remembering her tragic death in a car crash days before the film opened.

While Doodyville mourned the loss of the Princess, *The Mickey Mouse Club*, debuting in 1955 and starring the new heartthrob, Annette Funicello, closed in for the kill. By starting a half hour before *Howdy*, the Mouseketeers soon had *Howdy's* dinnertime audience switching over in droves. Despite *The Mickey Mouse Club's* popularity, the box, produced for the show's syndication in 1963, was a poor effort on the part of its unidentified artist.

For Milt Neil, the staid history lesson on the back of the *Howdy* box was a prophecy. Inexorably, the tone of Howdy's kid-vid successors, from ex-Clarabell Bob Keeshan's *Captain Kangaroo* through *Bozo the Clown* and *Shari Lewis*, was laundered of the inspired mayhem that marked Doodyville, save one.

Soupy Sales was the cream-pie-throwing exception. Surprised by his popularity, KST rushed midseason into the production of a vinyl Soupy lunch box. It hit the stores in January 1965, the same week Soupy hit the headlines by asking his young viewers to find their parents' wallets and mail him "those little green pieces of paper." The mad move may have delighted Mr. Bluster, but not network executives, who expelled Soupy from the airwaves. The lunch box sold out.

The Mickey Mouse Club, Aladdin Industries, 1963–67.
Although the show debuted in 1955, this box appeared with later syndication.

Captain Kangaroo, King Seeley Thermos, 1964–66.
Ex-Marine Bob Keeshan started his own show in 1955 after getting fired from *Howdy Doody,* where he played Clarabell. As in many vinyls kits, the bottle is more interesting than the box.

Shari Lewis, Aladdin Industries, 1963.

Soupy Sales, King Seeley Thermos, 1965.
What Miss Brooks could hold a handle to a classroom presence like this?

Bozo the Clown, Aladdin Industries, 1964–65.
Elmer Lehnhardt painted this attractive dome from TV's first
franchised clown show.

Mickey Mouse/Donald Duck, ADCO Liberty, 1954.
The box tradition of characters carrying their own lunch boxes probably began in
the Depression.

THE MOUSE'S PAILS

FIRST TO MERCHANDISE CHARACTER LUNCH pails back in the thirties, Disney was slow to develop the postwar market, waiting until 1954 to award ADCO Liberty, a small New Jersey metal-stamping firm, the license to produce a *Mickey Mouse/Donald Duck* kit.

Promoting Walt's just-completed amusement park, the *Disneyland* series debuted on television in 1955. Planned as *Disneyland* filler, *Davy Crockett* quickly turned into a craze that caught Disney with his pants down. Unlicensed Crockett merchandise sprang up everywhere. Leaping into action, ADCO Liberty produced a licensed *Davy Crockett* kit but committed heresy by spotlighting a non-Disney character, Kit Carson, on the back of the box. While shots from Davy's rifle rang out of the TV set, Walt's litigators swarmed like Santa Anna's army over the rabble responsible for the raft of knockoffs, including American Thermos (KST) for its *Davy Crockett* kit. "They hit us like a ton of bricks," says KST about the Crockett caper. "Overnight we pulled every box off the shelf." ADCO Liberty tried to redeem itself by creating an exclusive *Davy Crockett at the Alamo* box, but the earlier betrayal was not forgotten.

Aladdin copyrighted a *Daniel Boone* kit at the outbreak of the Crockett mania, hoping that it would have the same appeal as Davy's, but sat on it for another ten years, choosing instead to win over Walt's box business directly. (When KST came out in 1965 with a *Daniel Boone* kit, Aladdin, through the courts, had KST reissue it as *Fess Parker as Daniel Boone*.) Exploiting anger over ADCO's fumble and American Thermos's theft, Aladdin boxmen, over lunch, urged Disney to defect.

Thrown the bone in 1957, Aladdin launched a series of kits featuring lush postcard views of the Disneyland real estate. Using art supplied first by Walt's studios and then, once Walt realized they could do it as well, Aladdin's in-house talent, Aladdin sold over 25 million Disney kits by 1970.

Far and away the biggest single Disney seller, at 9 million kits, was the *Disney School Bus*, the brainchild of Disney "idea man" Al Konetzni. Konetzni waves off the difficulty of designing a lunch box as "take the best scene, put it on the first side, take the next best scene, put it on the second side," but the surviving trail of prototypes, including a black dome covered with colored balloons, suggests that's probably *hot air*.

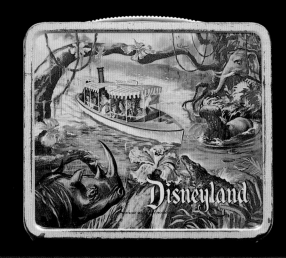

Aladdin's *Disneyland* boxes framed postcard views of Walt's heaven on earth.
(top left) *Disneyland* (castle), 1957–59. (top right) Back of castle box with Jungle
River ride. (bottom left) *Disneyland (Tomorrowland),* 1960–62. (bottom right)
Back of same *Tomorrowland* box.

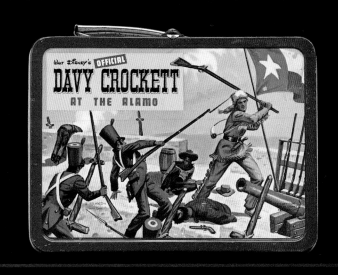

Faster than Davy could reload his rifle, the Crockett craze produced a raft of licensed and knockoff boxes. (top left) *Davy Crockett/Kit Carson,* ADCO Liberty, 1955. (top right) *Davy Crockett at the Alamo,* ADCO Liberty, 1955–56. (bottom left) *Daniel Boone,* Aladdin Industries, 1965. (bottom right) *Davy Crockett,* American Thermos, 1955–56.

ZORRO

ALADDIN INDUSTRIES, INCORPORATED, NASHVILLE

ZORRO
ALADDIN INDUSTRIES, INCORPORATED
NASHVILLE, TENN., U.S.A.

Ludwig Von Drake in Disneyland, Aladdin Industries, 1962.
Walt's poor opinion of highbrows is obvious in this atmospheric
jewel by Bob Burton.

Disney School Bus, Aladdin Industries, 1961–73.
The Disney executive in charge of the Aladdin account came up with this idea,
the biggest-selling kit in history. The presence of Goofy behind the wheel
explains the dents.

Gigi, Aladdin Industries, 1962–64.
Just a boxman's house dog the year before, Suzette, star of *Gigi,* was one more
proof of the American Dream.

GLAMOUR KITS

CAPTAINS OF INDUSTRY? SURE. MERCHANDISING visionaries? Of course. But as the "dainty little lady" boxes of the fifties illustrate, boxmen were, in Aladdin's words, "stumped about what to do for the little girls market." Until *Barbie* solved the problem by "selling millions per year after year," says KST, it was catch-as-catch-can.

Aware of their Achilles' heel, Aladdin's boxmen met regularly at the sales director's house. After work, they parked their big cars in his driveway and, over beer and barbecue, brainstormed for new products. The rub was coming up with their own characters, free from royalties, that would appeal to girls. Nipping at their ankles all the while was the sales director's poodle Suzette.

Once an idea hatched, "we made a few prototypes and the next day laid them out in front of the office secretaries for review," says Aladdin. "Usually the secretaries would just shake their heads." Undaunted, the boxmen pressed on. A few generic characters like *Junior Miss* did modestly well, "but overall we started to come under a lot of pressure to do a better job. Looking back, we were pretty dumb about it," admits Aladdin. "There was only one gal in the R&D section."

Around 1961 Aladdin's boxmen decided that they wanted a kit with a dog on it, probably a reaction to KST's vinyl *Poodle* kit. "Naturally, Vern [the sales director] insisted that it be Suzette," says Aladdin. "Never having had children, he thought the world of that pooch. He'd get *very* irate if anybody disturbed it. Once we were down at the house with a guy from the ad agency who accidentally rocked back in his chair on the dog . . . boy . . . Vern got so mad, we almost lost the agency. Another time a new salesman nearly killed the dog by feeding her a shrimp. Vern turned purple, pulled me out of the room, and whispered 'I want that fathead fired.'"

Groomed for success, Suzette moved up off the carpet onto vinyl in the 1962 pink *Gigi* kit, where Bob Burton featured her clicking her heels through romantic Paris. Later appearing on two *Suzette Brunch Bags*, she had a career that lasted well into the seventies. "It was tragic when she died," says Aladdin. "She's buried in a Nashville dog cemetery. Vern still visits the grave when he comes to town."

(top left) *Barbie*, King Seeley Thermos, 1962–64. (top right) *Barbie and Midge* dome, King Seeley Thermos, 1964–67. (bottom left) *Barbie and Francie*, King Seeley Thermos, 1966–70. (bottom right) *Skipper*, King Seeley Thermos, 1966–67.

Twiggy, Aladdin Industries, 1967–68.
Late in the season, boxmen threw together this kit to capitalize on the 17-year-old
cockney model's fashion conquest of America.

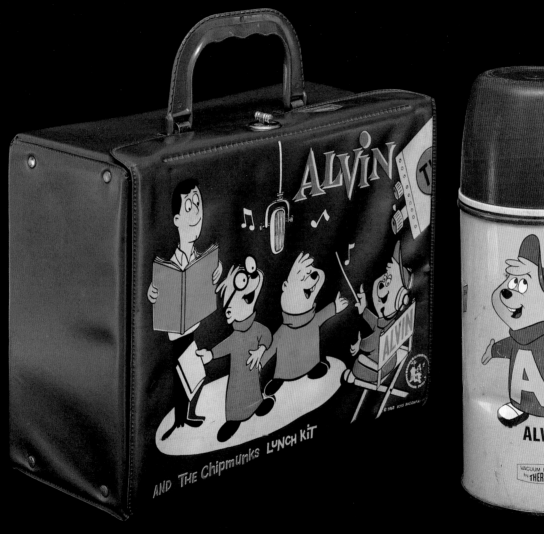

Alvin and the Chipmunks, King Seeley Thermos, 1963–64

ROCK-A-BUY BOXES

WHATEVER YOU THOUGHT OF ALVIN and the Chipmunks, they were the first rock colossi to grasp that lunch box sales, sandwiched between gold records and seasoned with dollops of TV exposure, were the building blocks to a lucrative personality cult. Pioneering new directions in marketing, their flesh and blood heirs to the charts, from the Fab Four to the Partridge Family, merely followed in their tracks.

Aladdin may have turned down the 'munks, but *damn* if they were going to lose *The Beatles* box. The day after the American debut of the Beatles on the *Ed Sullivan Show*, Aladdin dispatched a boxman to New York. "It was incredible chaos up in NEMS' New York hotel suite as hundreds of would-be merchandisers fought for a slice of the action. Nobody knew who controlled the property," he recalls. "NEMS [the Beatles' licensing arm] wanted twelve percent royalties. We *never* paid more than five percent, but after six months of camping there and pushing real hard, they came around."

Beating Aladdin by about a year were several vinyl *Beatles* boxes.

All were silkscreens based on the work of Beatles court photographer Dezo Hoffman. Although the Standard Plastics Products vinyl *Kaboodle* boxes probably were licensed, *The Beatles* Air Flite boxes, made in a Bronx loft, apparently were not. Neither brand featured a bottle.

Aladdin's beautiful blue steel box, painted by Elmer Lehnhardt from Dezo Hoffman's photographs, landed in the stores the same month John Lennon remarked that his group was "more popular than Jesus." The Bible Belt erupted into a firestorm of puritan indignation. From Texas to Virginia, the KKK wrenched any images of the blasphemers, including lunch boxes, out of the hands of dazed kids and burned them, nailed to crosses, at church rallies. Headquartered in the South, Aladdin was relieved when the controversy passed and retaliated by flooding more boxes into the crater left by the Klan.

Ironically, artist Bob Burton, an Ed Sullivan fan, was shocked when the Beatles first appeared on the air. "I know we made *Beatles* lunch kits," he says, choking on the conflict, "but seeing them on the show with that hair . . . was . . . appalling."

The Beatles, Aladdin Industries, 1966–67.
This classic, painted by Elmer Lehnhardt, sold over six hundred thousand

The Beatles Kaboodle Kit, Standard Plastic Products, 1965 or 1966.
From the maker of KST's vinyl boxes, SPP *Kaboodle*s came in yellow, lavender, white, and blue. None had a bottle.

The Beatles, Air Flite, 1965 or 1966.
These vinyls probably were knocked out, unlicensed, in a Bronx loft.

Go-Go Brunch Bag, Aladdin Industries, 1966–67.

The Monkees, King Seeley Thermos, 1967.
ooking like "the Beatles run through a Xerox machine," according to one critic,
Mike, Peter, Micky, and Davy bob across Nick LoBianco's favorite box. He also
designed their guitar logo, as a favor to friends at NBC.

Yellow Submarine, King Seeley Thermos, 1969.
This box, by Nick LoBianco, is no more authentic than the actors' voices in the
feature-length cartoon. The sub was a getaway car for a merchandising heist
engineered behind the Beatles' feuding backs.

The Archies, Aladdin Industries, 1970–71.
Bob Montana's Riverdale High revelers sing the bubble gum music including "Sugar Sugar," that the Monkees rejected.

Banana Splits, King Seeley Thermos, 1970.
Hanna-Barbera's costumed ripoff of the Monkees was esteemed by Joey Ramone as "the greatest band of all time."

Tom Corbett, Space Cadet, Aladdin Industries, 1952–53.
On the bottle, Bob Burton painted the helmetless heroes standing in
the infinite backyard of space, as impervious to the vacuum around them as
they would be to mosquitos.

ORBITAL FOOD CONTAINERS

GIDDY FROM DESIGNING A GLITTERING fleet of spaceshiplike coffee shop interiors across the Midwest, Bob Burton painted "his own likeness as a helmetless cadet floating above the lunar surface," says Aladdin, on the 1954 *Tom Corbett, Space Cadet* box. "He would have been scot-free had the sales director not recognized him and exploded, 'You're not getting away with this.'" Aladdin's mission control may have scrubbed the artist's countertop walk but saved the kit's late-night life forms and dramatic, deep shadow scenery. In keeping with his coffee shop creativity, Burton set out a map of the solar system on the back of the box which, like a paper place mat, marked off comfortable distances between the planets as if they were franchises in the Big Boy chain.

Free-lancer John Polgreen, illustrator for *The Golden Book of Space Flight,* a boomer supermarket staple that laid out America's space agenda, created the beautiful blue *Astronaut* dome in 1960 for KST. His armada of sleek reentry rockets, glandular, interplanetary probes, and boilerplate spacemen hums like a crowded drive-in parking lot on a hot summer evening. A smash, the dome became the burger and fries of KST's space line until 1967.

Wally Wood, EC Comics top artist in the fifties and creator of the Freefall Ferris character for *MAD* magazine, picked up the tempo by creating two scorching Supermarionation classics: the *Supercar* kit for Universal and after that company folded in 1963, the lurid *Fireball XL5* for KST. The success of *Fireball* was lucky for KST since they were having problems with their *Orbit* box. John Glenn's star vehicle sold well until the *National Geographic* pointed out that the cutaway drawing of the *Mercury* capsule had been lifted from the pages of a recent issue, forcing KST to pull the kit.

On the road to producing *The Towering Inferno* movie, Irwin "Master of Disaster" Allen squeezed open a can of worms with his TV trilogy, *Voyage to the Bottom of the Sea, Lost In Space,* and *Land of the Giants.* Allen's ooze—the bottom of the barrel as far as science was concerned—nevertheless sparkled with nightmare plots and eye-popping landscapes that electrified Elmer Lehnhardt and Nick LoBianco, with brilliant results. Rarely were the talents of these two artists better realized than in these three brilliant "block o' schlock" boxes.

Tom Corbett, Space Cadet, Aladdin Industries, 1954–55.
Adopting the TV-screen lithographed box from American Thermos, Bob
Burton originally painted himself as a cadet floating above the moon.

Tom Corbett, Space Cadet, Aladdin Industries, 1954–55.
The solar system map on the box's back saved Junior Cadets the trip to the
Texaco station before extracurricular excursions.

Astronaut, King Seeley Thermos, 1961–66.
A beautiful box by free-lancer John Polgreen, who illustrated another supermarket
staple, *The Golden Book of Space Flight.*

Space Explorer, Aladdin Industries, 1960.
Elmer Lehnhardt painted this kit for the 1959 *Men into Space.* The first post-*Sputnik* TV series, doomed by defense department script approval, burned up during its first season.

NEW *Space Age Discoveries!*

KEEP LIQUIDS SAFER... LONGER...

CHILD'S LUNCH KITS

by UNIVERSAL

Wonderful conversation pieces for the school bus . . . and classroom chatter. But more important . . . they are rugged to stand playground action and contain great new 10 oz. thermal bottles . . . the result of space age research for airlines . . . hospitals . . . the armed forces. Liquids stay hot or cold up to a record-breaking 36 hours . . . and there are no interior seams to trap undesirable bacteria.

SPEED-SELLING TWIN DISPLAYS WITH ROCKET PUNCH
Off the counter and under their arms . . . with a quick stop at the cash register. New vitality for lunch box sales.

INTRODUCING THE *NEW* SPACE SPANNER VANGUARD IV THERMAL BOTTLE

NO. 1202 scientifically tested to withstand orbiting youngsters and to keep 10 oz. contents hot or cold up to a record-breaking 36 hours. Unbreakable case. New nose-cone cup.

INTRODUCING THE *NEW* U.S. SPACE CORPS LUNCH BOX

NO. 4202 WB for the imaginative to tune-in outer space and "listen" to the planets. Long-range instruments lithographed on metal.

Space-Ray Lunch Box display contains 6 metal U. S. Space Corps boxes — shpg. wgt. 8 lbs. — Space Spanner Moon Missile display has 12 Vanguard IV bottles — shpg. wgt. 11 lbs., or combination U.S. Space-Corps Metal Lunch Box — fitted with Vanguard IV Thermal Bottle. **NO. 4202**—12 in master carton—25 lbs. shpg. wgt.

EVERYONE FITTED WITH NEW UNIVERSAL THERMAL BOTTLES — BEST IN 50 YEARS!

LITTLE DUTCH MISS
Heart-warmingly decorated in traditional happy-talk symbols. Lithographed on metal with matching 10 oz. bottle.
NO. 4196C
12 in carton · 25 lbs. shpg. wgt.

CASEY JONES
For the junior engineer or engineeress — extra sized metal lithographed lunch box has extra room in domed cover . . . 10 oz. new-type Universal Thermal bottle.
NO. 4151B
12 in carton · 25 lbs. shpg. wgt.

U.S. Space Corp catalog page, Universal, 1961.
Universal's innovative entrance into the space race included the knife-switch instrument panel box and a finned plastic *Vanguard IV* bottle.

Orbit, King Seeley Thermos, 1963.
John Glenn's star vehicle was dropped after *National Geographic* pointed out that an unidentified artist had lifted the cutaway capsule from the magazine's pages.

Supercar, Universal, 1962–63.
The legendary Wally Wood from EC Comics and *MAD* magazine painted this kit
for the syndicated British Supermarionation puppet show. The car, the logical
extreme of fifties' automotive styling, was the obvious foil to Ralph *Unsafe at
Any Speed* Nader's crusade.

Fireball XL5, King Seeley Thermos, 1964–65.
Another Supermarionation import painted by Wally Wood. Steve Zodiac and
Venus model in front of their blowtorch "get about" and Space City, both of which
look taken from the 1933 world's fair.

Captain Astro production sheet and box, Ohio Art Company, 1966–67.
The makers of Etch-A-Sketch invented this character in 1960 for a line of space
toys that included the featured red ray gun. Jess Hager, a free-lancer, also painted
the *Bond XX* box.

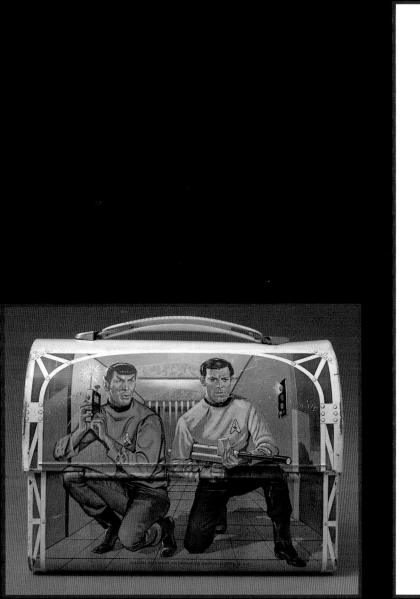

Star Trek, Aladdin Industries, 1968–69.
The *Enterprise,* its light-drenched bridge evoking Camelot's round table, warps
across the dome. On the end, Kirk and Spook impatiently wait for a table at
Denny's. One-quarter million kits were made and sold for around $3.50 each.

Lost In Space, King Seeley Thermos, 1967–68.
Barred from his usual Mondrian-like fixes because of the shape of the kit, and given only a few black and white glossies for inspiration, Nick LoBianco pulled his vibrant masterpiece out from some East River in his imagination. The Robinsons' "chariot" heads for cover under a comet-streaked sky. On the box's back, Don West saves Will and Penny from aggressive grass in *Jupiter II*'s front yard.

Voyage to the Bottom of the Sea, Aladdin Industries, 1967.
A malevolent mollusk gives the Flying Sub a scare on this humdinger of a box
Elmer Lehnhardt painted for the series about a research submarine, the *Seaview*,
that had a genius for attracting protoplasmic trouble. Admiral Nelson (Richard
Basehart) and Captain Crane (David Hedison) hang tough on the back, despite the
trademark rivet-splitting seizures.

Land of the Giants, Aladdin Industries, 1969–70.
The jungle green of Elmer Lehnhardt's box evokes the nightmare of nature (and Asian policing actions) gone amok. Coinciding with news coverage from Vietnam, the series about a world where the normal order is psychotically inverted might be a metaphor for that war. The billboard-sized Ho Chi Minh stand-in "goochy-gooing" the indignant plane crash survivors is artist Lehnhardt himself.

LAND OF THE GIANTS

© 1968 Kent Productions
20th Century Fox Film Corp.

ALADDIN INDUSTRIES, INCORPORATED NASHVILLE, TENN.

Superman, Universal, 1954–55.
Wayne Boring, the Man of Steel's comic strip artist in the fifties, created
this art. Boxmen didn't think TV actor George Reeves was a strong enough
presence to sell.

"HOLY PAILS, BOXMAN"

Superman **bottle, King Seeley Thermos, 1967–68.**
Nick LoBianco illustrated the kit when Superman came to Saturday morning as a cartoon.

"LOOK, UP IN THE SKY" made sense to *Superman* audiences in the fifties. They expected deliverance to arrive from above. But by the sixties, what dropped out of the sky might be the bomb, so action heroes such as Batman and the Green Hornet took to the streets. One incarnation, Flipper, even took to the water.

For most baby boomers, George Reeves, Superman on the original TV series, was the definitive Man of Steel. But it wasn't always so. Back in 1954, boxmen at Universal figured the comic strip had superior selling power, so they had comic strip artist Wayne Boring create the *Superman* box art rather than picturing that Johnny-come-lately Reeves. When a *Superman* cartoon series appeared on Saturday morning, Reeves had been dead for nine years. KST marketed the kit this time, with cartoon style artwork by Nick LoBianco.

By the midsixties, Batman, Bob Kane's 1939 comic strip character who once wrapped victims in his cape and killed them, came to TV, too. Stripped of his mysterious powers, the new Batman indulged in ridiculous costume drama that poked fun at himself. This new treatment utterly confused most boxmen. KST passed on the property and the licensor turned to Aladdin in 1965. "We sat down at home and watched the show," says Aladdin. "We thought it was one of the dumbest shows we had ever seen. We didn't realize it was *camp.* We told the licensor it *stank,* and he, running out of takers, replied 'You son of a bitch, you don't deserve it, but you've got it.'" To Aladdin's amazement, a million kits per year sold for two years.

The lesson of *Batman*'s producers was lost on *The Green Hornet,* who followed on his televised heels. The character was created in the forties by George Trendle, who had brought us the Lone Ranger. In fact, the Green Hornet, aka Britt Reid, was supposed to be the masked man's grandnephew. However, the series didn't "send up" its characters as *Batman* had done, and today is remembered more as the TV vehicle of late martial arts star Bruce Lee. Another forties' character played too straight in the sixties for its own good was Edgar Rice Burroughs's Tarzan.

Ivan Tors, creator of *Sea Hunt,* made a splash with *Flipper* in 1964. A creature cut from the heroic mold if ever there was one, this sea-going Lassie, played by a dolphin named Susie and painted by Nick LoBianco, wore another kind of mask more terrifying than those of his costumed cousins—an uncanny resemblance to Bob Hope! For flower-power Flipper, the new kryptonite was pollution.

Batman, Aladdin Industries, 1966–67.
Elmer Lehnhardt's *Batbox* is closer in spirit to Bob Kane's 1939 comic book
character that wrapped victims in his cape and killed them, than to the camp TV
series that had Hollywood stars lining up to be guest villains.

The Green Hornet, King Seeley Thermos, 1967.
"Faster, Kato!" Nick LoBianco captures the crusading publisher and his sidekick,
played by the late martial arts expert Bruce Lee, in the stinging act.

Tarzan, Aladdin Industries, 1967–68.
Artist John Henry catches Ron Ely—the fourteenth actor to play Edgar Rice
Burroughs's apeman—in the kind of scrap that made it a *demanding* role.

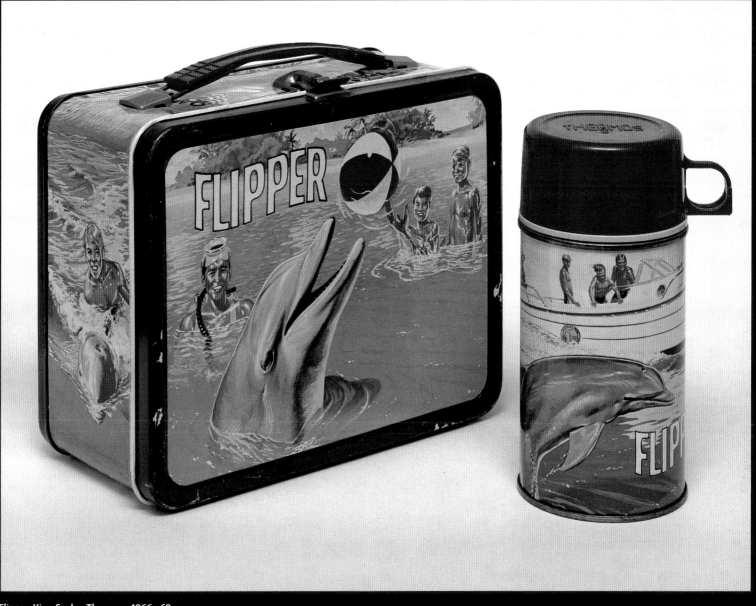

Flipper, King Seeley Thermos, 1966–68.
This seagoing Lassie, played by a dolphin named Susie, did well by Nick
LoBianco's flattering portrait. What more of a mask could you ask for than
Flipper's uncanny resemblance to Bob Hope?

Porky's Lunch Wagon, American Thermos, 1959–61.
Did this pit stop for the prime-time *Bugs Bunny Show* ensemble stand in the
Warner Brothers lot?

KIT-TOONS

BY THE LATE FIFTIES, THE TV networks realized that cartoons were the cheapest way to fill airtime. Like Wimpy's hamburger hunger, the networks' appetite for cartoon kiddie fodder was insatiable. With potential profits too small to make new, labor-intensive cartoons for the pocket change the networks paid, old studios such as Warner Brothers and King Features bundled up thirty years of sumptuous theatrical shorts and sold them to TV as a few hour-long shows. After *The Bugs Bunny Show* and *Popeye* aired in prime time, these studios folded, leaving the boxes, like the *Loonie Tunes TV Set* and *Popeye,* as tombstones to the old tradition.

Sensing an huge opportunity in the TV market, Bill Hanna and Joe Barbera, creators of *Tom and Jerry* cartoons in the forties, invented "limited" animation. Using static backgrounds and broad-lined characters, they pioneered a method whereby cartoons could be quickly made at one-tenth the previous cost. *Ruff and Reddy* was first off the assembly line, but in 1960 *The Flintstones,* an animated version of *The Honeymooners,* catapulted Hanna-Barbera to the top of the heap. Next year *The Jetsons* gave prime-time viewers a satirical look at how we would be living in the gadget-filled twenty-first century. Seeing the future, other surviving animators immediately adopted the streamlined style.

The new technique made life simpler for animators, but not necessarily for box artists. In 1961, Bob Clampett's *Beany & Cecil* puppets were animated for Saturday morning. Clampett, who created the character of Tweetie Pie at Warner Brothers, made himself into "a problem" at KST by scorning Nick LoBianco's suggested box designs for six months. Not much happier than LoBianco, Elmer Lehnhardt complained about "copy work" as he tortured George, Jane, and their Skypad Apartments to fit the *The Jetsons* kit, the only cartoon dome Aladdin ever made.

Fortunately for us, Lehnhardt threw the 1964 *Flintstones* box to a free-lancer named John Henry. A superb colorist, Henry, who later created the *James Bond* and *Tarzan* kits, bathed Bedrock's best in a brilliance worthy of Matisse.

Loonie Tunes TV Set, American Thermos, 1959–61.

Popeye, King Seeley Thermos, 1964–67.
Wally Wood's potent colors make us wish every box artist ate his spinach.

Through the (convertible Bullwinkle and Rocky Jay Ward Production] six de

Of these sixties' cartoons, only *Peanuts* endured longer than the average vinyl box.

(top left) *Beany & Cecil,* King Seeley Thermos, 1963. (top right) *Linus the Lionhearted,* Aladdin Industries, 1965. (bottom left) *Peanuts,* King Seeley Thermos, 1969. (bottom right) *Deputy Dawg,* King Seeley Thermos, 1961, 62.

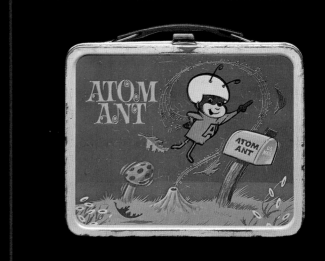

Illustrated by the hailstorm of pails, Hanna-Barbera dominated both prime-time and Saturday morning cartoons throughout the sixties. (top left) *Huckleberry Hound/Quick Draw McGraw,* Aladdin Industries, 1961–62. (top right) *Yogi Bear and Friends,* Aladdin Industries, 1963. (bottom left) *Cartoon Zoo Lunch Chest,* Universal, 1962. (bottom right) *Atom Ant,* King Seeley Thermos, 1966.

The Jetsons, Aladdin Industries, 1963.
Two weeks after premiering in prime time, Hanna-Barbera's look at the twenty-first century was eclipsed by the Cuban Missile Crisis, which made us wonder if we might not reach the suborbital suburbs. Elmer Lehnhardt's kit is encircled by scenes of the gadget-filled day of the first family of the future.

The Flintstones, Aladdin Industries, 1964–65.
The *Honeymooners* never had it so good. Artist John Henry's breathtaking box, the second for the longest-running cartoon in TV history, signals the arrival of Pebbles and Bamm Bamm to Bedrock.

Hector Heathcote, Aladdin Industries, 1964.
The Terrytoons adventure about a time traveler visiting milestones in history went to TV in 1963.

Dick Tracy, Aladdin Industries, 1967.
The square-jawed detective out of Chester Gould's famous strip entered Saturday cartoons in the early sixties.

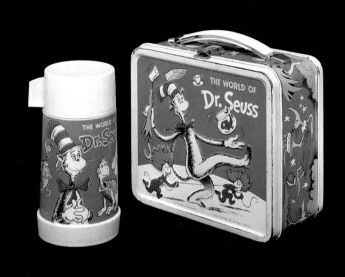

Dr. Seuss, Aladdin Industries, 1970–71.
The Doctor did the artwork on this, his greatest hit kit.

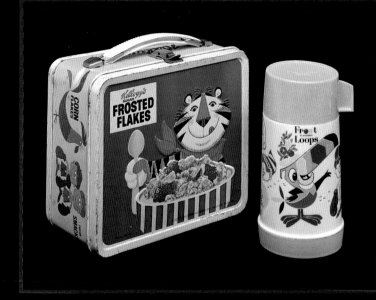

Kellogg's Breakfast, Aladdin Industries, 1969.
The cereal maker wanted sample boxes put in every kit, but boxmen, fearing weevils would attack the warehouse, said no.

Steve Canyon, Aladdin Industries, 1959.
Milton Caniff, famed for bringing realism to the comic strip, created this kit for his
short-lived TV series. "All the art was based on photos," the superb draughtsman
said, adding, "No, I did not resemble Canyon."

BATTLE KITS

AS *SPUTNIK*, ACTUALLY NO BIGGER than a lunch box itself, upped the cold war ante by menacing Old Glory from orbital high ground, patriotic boxmen fired a flurry of chest-beater boxes into the supermarkets to reassure kids that Uncle Sam was minding the store. Perfect for cans of distilled water and civil defense biscuits, these duck 'n' cover icons were as much a part of the curriculum as the "Pledge of Allegiance," fallout drills, and wearing immolation-proof ID bracelets.

Best of the bunch is Milton Caniff's 1959 *Steve Canyon* kit, for it captures the terrifying and titillating defense schizophrenia of the time. The box shows the square-jawed hero standing under blue skies in front of his aluminum war-horse while the bottle telegraphs the consequences of lapsed vigilance—a global fire storm of orange ICBM exhaust and mushrooming clouds. Canyon's mile-long stare reads like the iconic "Only you can prevent . . ." of Smokey the Bear.

The pragmatic Caniff liked that *Canyon* box "best of the fifty-six items licensed for the TV series not only because I carried a box, not so well appointed, in grammar school, but because its sales made it possible for me to eat at 21 [Manhattan's swank restaurant]."

Twelve miles inland from America's chief submarine construction yard and base on the Connecticut coast, KST got into the act by enlisting the help of its neighbor, General Dynamics. The huge defense contractor obligingly forked over drawings of its latest engineering marvels, including the first ballistic missile–firing sub, which an unknown artist converted into the *Submarine* box.

By the early sixties, with news of Vietnam still buried in the back pages, Cold War posturing gave way to a rash of hot war dramas on TV. Now that the Second World War was at a "safe" historical distance, producers began to re-create the last "good fight" for evening viewing. Of these shows, only *The Rat Patrol*, whose leapin' jeeps merged the blue-collar love of off-road adventure with the taste of blood, was boxed.

A few years later, Vietnam was coming forward into the headlines, and gung ho *GI Joe*, a kit for the extremely popular Hasbro action doll, flirted with the war. The Joe box's tour of duty lasted two years before falling casualty to a changing tide of public opinion toward the war.

Jet Patrol, Aladdin Industries, 1957–58.
A late-night sign-off flyby featuring the flower and some of the fudge of the
nation's air defense. *Pogo*, the experimental aircraft on the bottle, couldn't safely
lift its own weight.

Submarine, King Seeley Thermos, 1960–63.
More important than being America's first ballistic sub, the *Seawolf* reportedly
boasted the first electric organ in the silent service.

The Rat Patrol, Aladdin Industries, 1967–68.
Rommel would have enjoyed Elmer Lehnhardt's box for the popular
leapin' jeeps TV series, filmed in Spain with hardware left over from the
Battle of the Bulge movie.

Battle Kit, King Seeley Thermos, 1965–66.
A generic for the rash of Second World War IV shows.

GI Joe, King Seeley Thermos, 1967–68.
Introduced in 1964, Hasbro's action doll is shown rehearsing for the mining of
Haiphong harbor.

The Munsters, King Seeley Thermos, 1965.
Nick LoBianco captures your typical family, living your typical daydream: Funeral
director Herman (Fred Gwynne) is "turned on" by his wife (Yvonne DeCarlo)

KIT COMEDY

RUMORS ABOUND BUT THE *Leave it to Beaver* show never had a lunch box. During the opening credits of the early episodes, the Beav carried a plain box. When asked about it as an adult, Jerry Mathers replied in kind of a "Gee Wally" way, "I don't really remember. . . . I was just a kid. I never thought I'd have to comment on lunch boxes later in life." Indeed.

A far cry from the well-rehearsed morality tale of *Beaver, The Beverly Hillbillies* did have a box. Faddish, gimmicky, and aimed low at kids, sitcoms of the sixties were ideal for merchandising. Exwrestler Elmer Lehnhardt delighted in incorporating sight gags into his comedy kits, and more often than not, the results proved better than a backyard oil well for Aladdin.

The Munsters, a series created by the same team that brought us *Leave it to Beaver,* was KST's first sitcom smash. *The Munsters,* like the competing *Addams Family,* spoofed the monster craze that gripped the nation following Universal Studios' sale of classic horror films to TV. Nick LoBianco's box, with its scene of Herman Munster about to be "turned on" by his wife, is more in the Lehnhardt tradition than his later comedy kits, which were made too hurriedly to develop sticky situations.

Naturally, the *Munsters* box has a ghost story. Hours before the midnight deadline for the original art, LoBianco had his younger brother drive the finished art up to KST's Connecticut plant. "It was a terrific storm . . . with lightning flashes and thunderclaps," says Peter LoBianco. "I felt I had moved into that goddamn show. Coming down that twisting Thames River gorge, the rain coming down so hard it broke the wipers, so there I was with my head out the window, drenched, trying to steer. I pulled up to the guardhouse one minute before twelve. I was creeped out getting out of the car because the plant, with its huge gothic silhouette, looked like Herman Munster's mansion."

On another errand, this time to deliver the art for *Laugh-In*'s hillbilly cousin, LoBianco's brother "dropped off the art on the desk of the show's New York producer, who was busy on the phone. Returning to the elevator, I knew it was found and *approved* when a high pitched 'HEE HAW' broke from the office."

As an exwrestler, Elmer Lehnhardt had an approach to comedy that was always muscular and full of surprises. Here are four wonderful sitcom boxes he created for Aladdin, loaded with sight gags. (top left) *The Beverly Hillbillies,* 1963–65. (top right) *The Flying Nun,* 1968–69. (bottom left) *Gomer Pyle,* 1966. (bottom right) *Gentle Ben,* 1968–69.

Hogan's Heroes, Aladdin Industries, 1966.
Lehnhardt brings Stalag 13 to life. Colonel Hogan (Bob Crane), Colonel Klink, LeBeau, Newkirk, and Kinchloe hug the only hilarious quonset hut of the Second World War.

It's About Time, Aladdin Industries, 1967.
Lehnhardt created this stone Swiss cheese for the CBS answer to *Lost In Space,* starring Imogene Coca. Time ran out on the culture-clash comedy about Gemini astronauts in a time warp meeting their Stone Age ancestors before the kit hit the stores, a disaster for Aladdin that "sickened us on space."

Nick LoBianco, partial to abstraction, approached humor by creating a scene that evoked the comedy of the original broadcast. Brushed out at a gallop, his boxes often lack the choreographed devices used by Lehnhardt. Here are four boxes LoBianco created for KST in the sixties.

(top left) *Julia*, 1969–70. (top right) *Family Affair*, 1969–70. (bottom left) *The Brady Bunch*, 1970. (bottom right) *Hee Haw*, 1970–71.

Laugh-In, Aladdin Industries, 1969.
Elmer Lehnhardt's superb artistry is obvious here on the portraits of Dick Martin and the late Dan Rowan. Their psychedelic comedy "happening" introduced many unknowns, including Goldie Hawn and Lily Tomlin.

Laugh-In, Aladdin Industries, 1970.
Proof for some that baby boomers refused to grow up, one of the show's original sight gags—an adult in a rain slicker pedaling a tricycle— explodes out of Lehnhardt's psychedelic box.

James Bond—Agent 007, Aladdin Industries, 1966.
The high-octane *Thunderball* scenes by free-lancer John Henry kicked off the
school-yard spy scene.

COLD CUT WARRIORS

NO STRANGER TO INTRIGUES OF the heart, JFK fathered the phenomenon by mentioning to a reporter that *From Russia with Love* was a favorite book. *Life* magazine picked up the story, and faster than you could count 007, the spy craze swept coast to coast. Boxes savor the whole sordid *affair* as it spiraled, ever more satirically, down the decade.

Although queasy about film kits, because "the hoopla was usually over by the time the box came out," Aladdin was convinced to license a pail by the succession of smash Bond films. The *James Bond–Agent 007* box hit the stores in 1966, shadowed by a couple of knockoffs, Ohio Art's *Bond XX* and KST's *Secret Agent.*

Mutating into parody, *The Man from U.N.C.L.E.* and *Get Smart* slipped spies into the small screen. Whereas *U.N.C.L.E.* was played as camp by its smirking cast—though young audiences missed the droll one-liners and saw only suspenseful drama—the tone of Mel Brooks's *Get Smart* was unmistakable. KST bought both properties but could have managed one better. "*Get Smart* would have been the best kit we ever had, but we *got stupid* instead of smart . . . and discontinued it after two years. It would have been a runaway barn-burner."

The Man from U.N.C.L.E. kit was roughed out by Nick LoBianco but finished by Jack Davis, a name commercial artist long involved with EC Comics and *MAD* magazine, as well as painting thirty-six *Time* magazine covers during the Watergate spill. When told that the original *U.N.C.L.E.* box art, created in the spirit of his *It's a Mad, Mad, Mad, Mad World* movie poster, had been thrown out, Davis said stoically in his Atlanta drawl, "I don't cry over it. God has been good to me."

Not quite as blessed, the trend reached its lowest point (and probably the widest audience) in 1970 with a simian version of *Get Smart* called *Lance Link, Secret Chimp.*

Secret Agent, King Seeley Thermos, 1968–69.
The decoder on the back of the box, featuring tools of the cloak and dagger trade, was Nick LoBianco's idea.

The Man from U.N.C.L.E., King Seeley Thermos, 1966–67.
Napoleon Solo and Illya Kuryakin look out of their minds. They should: *MAD*'s
Jack Davis did the illustration.

Get Smart, King Seeley Thermos, 1966–67.
Nick LoBianco's kit for Mel Brooks's beloved spy spoof, starring Don Adams and
Barbara Feldon as CONTROL agents 86 and 99.

Lance Link, Secret Chimp, King Seeley Thermos, 1971.
The satirical spy spiral ended here.

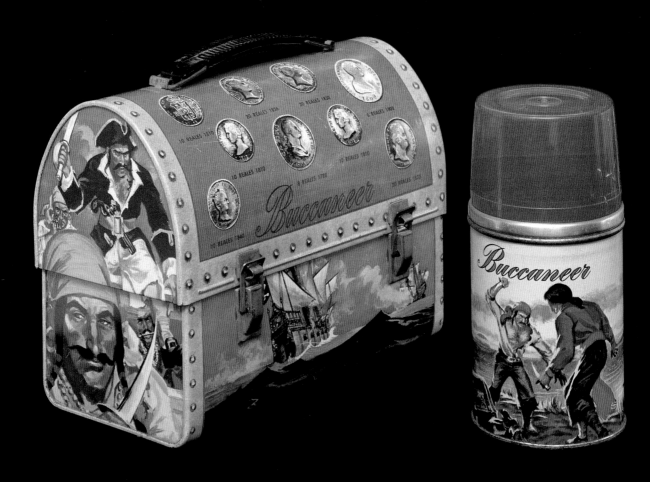

Buccaneer, Aladdin Industries, 1957–58.
Bob Burton's brilliant muzzle-flash orange and emerald green pirate chest looks
like one of his fantastic coffee shop interiors turned inside out. On the sly, Burton
painted his profile on two ten reales coins in the vault.

HOME OF THE DOMES

TYPICALLY, BOTH ALADDIN AND KST deny the other credit for inventing the decorated dome.

As Aladdin tells it, "Kids wanted a box like their fathers would carry but in smaller sizes, so we made a tiny black dome box back in the midfifties. Then it hit us in 1956, why not lithograph those, too, put a theme on them? I think Burton's first was a treasure chest. We called it *Buccaneer.*" Aladdin fails to mention that the object that "hit us" probably was the 1956 TV series called *The Buccaneers* starring young Robert Shaw of later *Jaws* fame.

"Hell no, *we* were first," snorts KST, "our *Red Barn* [a generic designed to beat the high cost of licensed character kit royalties] was already on the R & D department's drawing table back in 1956." Contrary to this *Pravda* line, KST "deep throats" whisper that the idea was really derived from a workman's dome painted red and black to look like a barn that arrived unsolicited from a Michigan woman. When the mass-produced *Red Barn* made its retail debut in 1957, she sued, and the dispute was settled out of court.

Regardless of whether Aladdin or KST flew the Jolly Roger, the ensuing dome war challenged boxmen to go for broke. Although cannon fire from Burton's *Buccaneer* filled the supermarket with smoke and left American Thermos's original *Red Barn* burning to the ground, Thermos rushed in *Firehouse* to put out the flames. Taken aback by Thermos's building a better *Red Barn* on the ashes, Aladdin circled its *Chuck Wagons,* and so on. A break from the tyranny of the TV screen box, domes electrified imaginations perhaps better than any other type of box.

For many boxmen, the deadpan *Pop Art Bread Box* of the late sixties was the final word. The aesthetic movement pioneered by Andy Warhol had elevated the mundane, and Aladdin returned the compliment by creating the ultimate lunch box whose form reflected what it carried. Kids thought the whole idea dumb, though, and the kit, with its Campbell's soup bottle, molded on shelves.

Watch those fingers, that's one mean shark patrolling Davy Jones's locker.

While Aladdin's *Buccaneer* terrorized the coastline, American Thermos concentrated its dome power on small-town Americana. (bottom) *Red Barn*, 1958–50.

Firehouse catalog page, American Thermos, 1959–60.

Hometown Airport, King Seeley Thermos, 1960.
Ed Wexler created this high-flying dome that today is among the
rarest of the domes.

Circus Wagon, American Thermos, 1958.
The sign on the monkey cage of the bottle reads "Warning, Do Not
Stand Too Close."

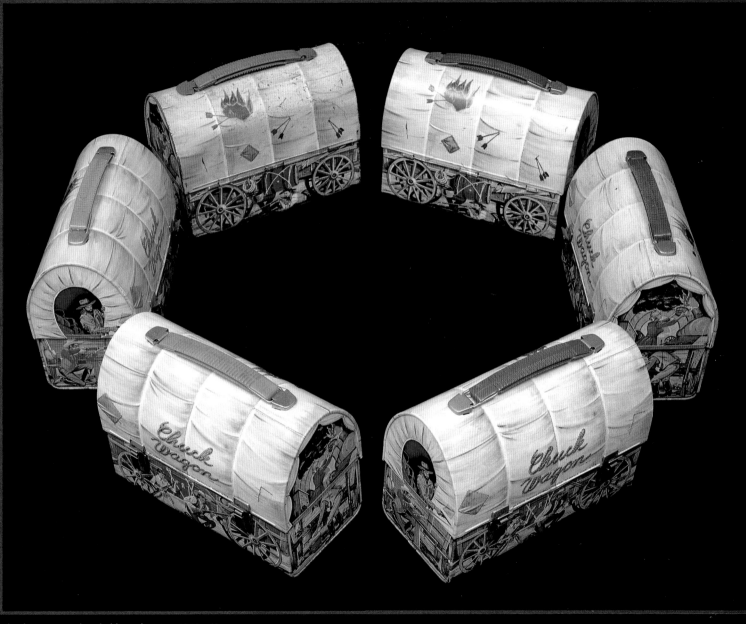

Chuck Wagon circle, Aladdin Industries, 1958–60.
Judging from the scene, somebody must be pretty mad about the food. The dome
was Bob Burton's next after *Buccaneer*.

Globetrotter, Aladdin Industries, 1959–60.
This is the best of many sticker-covered luggage kits.

Treasure Chest, Aladdin Industries, 1961–62.
Probably a lot of these shelf-paper versions of *Buccaneer* were buried.

Cable Car, Aladdin Industries, 1962.
Could inspiration have come from anywhere other than Rice-A-Roni commercials?

Casey Jones, Universal, 1960–61.
An unlicensed locomotive for the *Casey Jones* TV series starring Alan Hale, who

Pop Art Bread Box, Aladdin Industries, 1968.
Kids found this pop art treasure unappetizing and left the box to mold
on store shelves.

Appendix:

SELECTED BOX RARITY AND ARTIST IDENTIFICATION TABLE

 THIS TABLE LISTS OVER TWO hundred easily identifiable lunch boxes manufactured in the United States between 1950 and the early 1970s (TV series such as *The Partridge Family* debuted in the late sixties but were not boxed for several years). Each box is rated on a scale from one to twenty; the higher the number, the rarer the item. A value of twenty is assigned to any box without a known surviving example. Bottles are not listed, but should be valued, particularly those from rare vinyl kits, two or three points below the corresponding box. Note that (1) American Thermos after 1959 becomes King Seeley Thermos (KST); (2) boxes not specifically listed as dome or vinyl are "flat" steel (the familiar rectangular box); and (3) only prominent examples of box families, such as *Roy Rogers*, are listed.

A column identifies, whenever possible, the artist or artists responsible for creating each listed box. Frequently one artist roughed out a lunch box design, then turned it over to another artist to complete the artwork. This was often the case with Aladdin's Burton and Lehnhardt team. In the table, this collaboration is designated by listing the initials of both artists, designer first.

Key to artist initials:

AK	Al Konetzni
CB	Charlie Brown (free-lancer)
DS	Disney Studios
EL	Elmer Lehnhardt
EW	Ed Wexler
HP	Herb Plassmann
JB	Jim Blackburn (free-lancer)
JD	Jack Davis
JH (if Ohio Art)	Jess Hager (free-lancer)
JH (if Aladdin)	John Henry (free-lancer)
JM	Jock Marshall (free-lancer)
JP	John Polgreen (free-lancer)
MC	Milton Caniff
MN	Milt Neil
NLB	Nick LoBianco
RB	Robert O. Burton
RL	Rinaldo Leverone (free-lancer)
SA	Sally Augustini
TG	Theodore Geisel (Dr. Seuss)
TO	T. Oughton (free-lancer)
WB	Wayne Boring
WW	Wally Wood

Name	Date	Maker	Type	Artist	Value
Airline	'68–69	Ohio Art		HP	14
All Star	'60	Aladdin	vinyl	?	18
All-American (U.S. map)	'54–55	Universal		?	18
Alvin and the Chipmunks	'63–64	KST	vinyl	NLB	17
Americana (48 states)	'58–63	American Thermos		JM	18
Annie Oakley	'56–58	Aladdin		RB	16
The Archies	'70–71	Aladdin		JB	11
Astronaut	'61–66	KST	dome	JP	16
The Astronauts	'70–71	Aladdin		EL	13
Atom Ant	'66	KST		NLB	16
Auto Race	'67–70	KST		NLB	14
Ballerina	'60–63	Aladdin	vinyl	?	19
Ballet	'61	Universal	vinyl	?	20
Banana Splits	'70	KST	vinyl	NLB	17
Barbie	'62–64	KST	vinyl	CB/NLB	16
Barbie and Francie	'66–70	KST	vinyl	NLB	15
Barbie and Midge	'64–65	KST	vinyl	NLB	16
Barbie and Midge dome	'64–67	KST	vinyl	NLB	19
Batman	'66–67	Aladdin		EL	15
Battle Kit	'65–66	KST		NLB/TO	14
Beany & Cecil (white)	'62	KST	vinyl	NLB	18
Beany & Cecil (brown)	'63	KST	vinyl	NLB	18
The Beatles	'65–66	Air Flite	vinyl	—	17
The Beatles	'66–67	Aladdin		EL	14
The Beatles Brunch Bag	'66	Aladdin	vinyl	EL	17
The Beatles Kaboodle Kit	'65–66	SPP	vinyl	—	18
The Beverly Hillbillies	'63–65	Aladdin		EL	14
Blondie	'69	KST		NLB/CB	15
Boating	'59–61	American Thermos		EW	19
Bobby Soxer	'59	Aladdin	vinyl	?	19
Bonanza (green rim)	'63–64	Aladdin		RB/EL	15
Bonanza (brown rim)	'65–66	Aladdin		RB/EL	15
Bonanza (yellow)	'68–69	Aladdin		EL	14
Bond XX	'66–67	Ohio Art		JH	18
Bozo the Clown	'64–65	Aladdin	dome	EL	16
The Brady Bunch	'70	KST		NLB	14
Brave Eagle	'56–57	American Thermos		EW	17
Buccaneer	'57–58	Aladdin	dome	RB	17
Bullwinkle and Rocky	'62	Universal		?	18
Bullwinkle (ballooning)	'62	KST	vinyl	CB	18
Bullwinkle (space)	'63	KST	vinyl	NLB	19
Cable Car	'62	Aladdin	dome	RB	18
Campus Queen	'67–71	KST		NLB	14
Captain Astro	'66–67	Ohio Art		JH	18
Captain Kangaroo	'64–66	KST	vinyl	NLB	17
Carousel	'65	Aladdin	vinyl	?	19
Cartoon Zoo Lunch Chest	'62	Universal		?	18
Casey Jones	'60–61	Universal	dome	?	18
Casper	'66	KST	vinyl	?	17
Chitty Chitty Bang Bang	'69	KST		?	14
Chuck Wagon	'58–60	Aladdin	dome	RB	16
Circus Wagon	'58	American Thermos	dome	?	18
Civil War	'61	Universal	plastic	?	20
Combo Brunch Bag	'67	Aladdin	vinyl	?	19
Corsage	'58–63	American Thermos		JM	15
Corsage	'63	KST		?	14
Corsage	'64–72	KST		?	15
Corsage	'70	KST	vinyl	?	17
Cowboy in Africa	'68	KST		NLB	16
Daniel Boone (copyrighted '55)	'65	Aladdin		RB/EL	16
Davy Crockett	'55–56	American Thermos		EW	15
Davy Crockett at the Alamo	'55–56	ADCO Liberty		?	16
Davy Crockett/Kit Carson	'55	ADCO Liberty		?	16
Deputy Dawg	'61–62	KST	vinyl		18
Dick Tracy	'67	Aladdin		RB/EL	15
Disney Fire Truck	'69–71	Aladdin	dome	EL	13
Disney School Bus	'61–73	Aladdin	dome	AK/EL	11
Disneyland (castle)	'57–59	Aladdin		RB	16
Disneyland (Tomorrowland)	'60–62	Aladdin		RB	17
Doctor Dolittle	'68–69	Aladdin		EL	14
Dr. Seuss	'70	Aladdin	vinyl	TG	18
Dr. Seuss	'70–71	Aladdin		TG	15
Dudley Do Right	'63	Universal		?	17
Dutch Cottage	'58	American Thermos	dome	?	19
Family Affair	'69–70	KST		NLB	14
Fess Parker Kaboodle Kit	'65	SPP	vinyl	?	19
Fess Parker as Daniel Boone	'66	KST		NLB/TO	14
Fireball XL5	'64–65	KST		CB/WW	16
Fire Station	'59–60	American Thermos	dome	?	16
Flag-o-rama (U.N. flags)	'54–55	Universal		?	18
The Flintstones	'64–65	Aladdin		JH	16
The Flintstones & Dino	'62	Aladdin		RB/EL	14
Flipper	'66–68	KST		NLB	14
The Flying Nun	'68–69	Aladdin		EL	14
The Flying Nun Brunch Bag	'68–69	Aladdin	vinyl	EL	19
Frontier Days	'57–59	Ohio Art		?	17
Gene Autry	'54–55	Universal		?	17

Name	Date	Maker	Type	Artist	Value	Name	Date	Maker	Type	Artist	Value
Gentle Ben	'68–69	Aladdin		EL	14	Lunch 'n Munch (raft)	'59–60	American Thermos	vinyl	?	20
Get Smart	'66–67	KST		NLB	14	Lunch 'n Munch (space)	'59–60	American Thermos	vinyl	?	20
GI Joe	'67–68	KST		NLB	14	Mam'zelle	'70–71	Aladdin	vinyl	SA	17
Gigi	'62–64	Aladdin	vinyl	RB	17	The Man from U.N.C.L.E.	'66–67	KST		JD	15
Globetrotter (luggage)	'59–60	Aladdin	dome	RB	17	Mary Poppins	'65	Aladdin		RB	16
Go-Go	'66–67	Aladdin	vinyl	?	19	Mary Poppins Brunch Bag	'66–67	Aladdin	vinyl	EL	19
Go-Go Brunch Bag	'66–67	Aladdin	vinyl	?	19	Mickey Mouse/Donald Duck	54–55	ADCO Liberty		DS	16
Gomer Pyle	'66	Aladdin		EL	15	The Mickey Mouse Club (yellow rim)	'63–67	Aladdin		DS	13
Great Wild West (Indian on horse)	'59–60	Universal		?	18	Mickey Mouse Kaboodle Kit	'64	SSP	vinyl	?	19
The Green Hornet	'67	KST		NLB	16	Minnie Mouse	pre-'65	SSP	vinyl	?	19
The Guns of Will Sonnett	'68	KST		NLB	16	The Monkees	'67	KST	vinyl	NLB	16
Gunsmoke (tan rim)	'59–61	Aladdin		RB/EL	15	The Monroes	'67	Aladdin		EL	17
Gunsmoke (red rim)	'62	Aladdin		RB/EL	16	Moon Landing	'68–69	Ardee Industries	vinyl	?	19
Hector Heathcote	'64	Aladdin		?	18	The Munsters	'65–66	KST		NLB	14
Hee Haw	'70–71	KST		NLB	13	N.F.L. Quarterback	'64	Aladdin		EL	16
Hogan's Heroes	'66	Aladdin	dome	EL	16	Orbit (Glenn's flight)	'63	KST		?	16
Hometown Airport	'60–61	KST	dome	EW	19	Paladin (Have Gun Will Travel)	'60	Aladdin		RB	15
Hopalong Cassidy	'54–56	Aladdin		RB	15	The Partridge Family	'71–74	KST		NLB	13
Hopalong Cassidy (decal)	'50–53	Aladdin		RB	14	Pathfinder (scout)	'59	Universal		?	19
Hot Wheels	'70–72	KST		NLB/RL	13	Patriotic (flag)	'70–71	Ohio Art		HP	13
Howdy Doody	'54–55	ADCO Liberty		MN	18	Peanuts (tan rim)	'66–72	KST		NLB	13
Huckleberry Hound	'61–62	Aladdin		RB	15	Peanuts (red)	'69	KST	vinyl	NLB	18
It's A Small World	'68–69	Aladdin	vinyl	?	18	Peter Pan	'69	Aladdin		EL	14
It's About Time	'67	Aladdin	dome	EL	17	Pets 'n Pals (Lassie/Fury)	'61–63	KST		?	16
James Bond–Agent 007	'66	Aladdin		JH	15	Playball	'69–72	KST		NLB	14
Jet Patrol	'57–58	Aladdin		RB	17	Ponytail—Eats 'n Treats	'59	KST	vinyl	?	18
The Jetsons	'63	Aladdin	dome	RB/EL	17	Ponytail—Tid Bit Kit	'59–63	KST	vinyl	?	17
Julia	'69–70	KST		NLB	14	Pop Art Bread Box	'68	Aladdin	dome	?	17
The Jungle Book	'68–69	Aladdin		EL	15	Popeye	'63	Universal		?	18
Junior Nurse	'63–64	KST	vinyl	NLB	19	Popeye	'64–67	KST		CB/WW	15
Kellogg's Breakfast	'69	Aladdin		EL	15	Porky's Lunch Wagon	'59–61	American Thermos	dome	?	16
Kewtie Pie	'64–67	Aladdin	vinyl	?	19	Psychedelic	'69	Aladdin	dome	?	16
Knight in Armor	'59–60	Universal		?	19	The Pussycats	'68–69	Aladdin	vinyl	?	17
Lance Link, Secret Chimp	'71	KST		NLB	13	The Pussycats Brunch Bag	'68–71	Aladdin	vinyl	?	18
Land of the Giants	'69–70	Aladdin		EL	15	The Rat Patrol	'67–68	Aladdin		RB/EL	14
Laugh-In (helmet back)	'69–70	Aladdin		EL	14	Red Barn (closed doors)	'57	American Thermos	dome	—	15
Laugh-In (tricycle)	'70	Aladdin		EL	16	Red Barn (open doors)	'58–60	American Thermos	dome	?	13
Laugh-In Brunch Bag	'70	Aladdin	vinyl	EL	17	The Rifleman	'61–62	Aladdin		RB/EL	17
Lawman	'61–62	KST		?	15	Ringling Brothers Circus	'70	KST	vinyl	NLB	18
Linus the Lionhearted	'65	Aladdin	vinyl	?	19	Road Runner	'70–73	KST		NLB	12
The Lone Ranger	'54–55	ADCO Liberty		?	17	Robin Hood	'56–58	Aladdin		RB	15
Lonnie Tunes TV Set	'59–61	American Thermos		?	16						
Lost in Space	'67–68	KST	dome	NLB	16						
Ludwig Von Drake in Disneyland	'62	Aladdin		RB	16						

Name	Date	Maker	Type	Artist	Value	Name	Date	Maker	Type	Artist	Value
Roy Rogers & Dale Evans (narrow box)	'53–54	American Thermos		EW	13	Tammy & Pepper	'65–67	Aladdin	vinyl	JH	19
Roy Rogers & Dale Evans (red shirt)	'57–59	American Thermos		EW	16	Tarzan	'67–68	Aladdin		RB/JH	16
Roy Rogers Chow Wagon	'58–61	American Thermos	dome	EW	17	Tinker Bell	'69	Aladdin	vinyl	SA	19
Roy Rogers Saddlebag (cream)	'61	KST	vinyl	?	18	Tom Corbett, Space Cadet (decal)	'52–53	Aladdin		RB	15
Roy Rogers Saddlebag (tan)	'60	KST	vinyl	?	16	Tom Corbett, Space Cadet	'54–55	Aladdin		RB	18
Satellite	'59–62	American Thermos		?	15	Train	'70–71	Ohio Art		HP	13
Secret Agent	'68–69	KST		NLB/?	15	Treasure Chest	'61–62	Aladdin	dome	EL	19
Shari Lewis	'63	Aladdin	vinyl	RB/EL	18	Trigger	'56	American Thermos		EW	17
Skipper	'66–67	KST	vinyl	NLB	18	Twiggy	'67–68	Aladdin	vinyl	EL	18
Sleeping Beauty	'70	Aladdin	vinyl	?	18	Twiggy Brunch Bag	'67–68	Aladdin	vinyl	EL	19
Smokey the Bear	'65	KST	vinyl	CB/NLB	19	U.S. Mail	'69–76	Aladdin	dome	JB	12
Snoopy's Doghouse	'69–72	KST	dome	NLB	13	U.S. Space Corp	'61	Universal		?	18
Soupy Sales	'65	KST	vinyl	NLB	19	Voyage to the Bottom of the Sea	'67	Aladdin		EL	16
Space Explorer	'60	Aladdin		EL	19	VW Bus	'60s	Omni Graphics	dome	?	17
Sports Afield	'57–61	Ohio Art		?	17	Wagon Train	'64–65	KST		NLB/CB	15
Star Trek	'68–69	Aladdin	dome	RB/EL	15	Wild Bill Hickok	'56–58	Aladdin		RB	14
Steve Canyon	'59	Aladdin		MC	15	Wild, Wild West	'69	Aladdin		EL	14
Stewardess	'62	Aladdin	vinyl	JH	19	Winnie the Pooh	'67	Aladdin		DS	16
Submarine	'60–63	KST		?	15	Winnie the Pooh	'67–68	Aladdin	vinyl	EL	19
Supercar	'62–63	Universal		WW	17	Wrangler	'62	Aladdin	vinyl	EL	19
Superman	'54–55	Universal		WB	18	Yellow Submarine	'69	KST		NLB	15
Superman	'67–68	KST		NLB	15	Yogi Bear	'64	Aladdin	vinyl	EL	19
Suzette Brunch Bag	'70–71	Aladdin	vinyl	?	17	Yogi Bear and Friends	'63	Aladdin		EL	16
Tammy	'64	Aladdin	vinyl	?	19	Zorro (black rim)	'58–59	Aladdin		RB	15
						Zorro (red)	'66	Aladdin		EL	17

ACKNOWLEDGMENTS

I'm grateful to the many individuals who helped bring this book to life. Among the box artists, whose anecdotes made it possible, I wish to thank Sally Augustini, Beverly Burge, Mr. and Mrs. Robert O. Burton, the late Milton Caniff, Jack Davis, Donald Henry, John Henry, Al Konetzni, Rinaldo Leverone, Milt Neil, Nick and Peter LoBianco.

My hearty thanks to boxmen George Cole, Vern Church, Paul Duevel, Don Eccleston, and Ed Nill for their reminiscences and memorabilia. Just as appreciated are Linda French, Victor Johnson, Dan Hosse, Mary Lou Miles, Barbara Nash at Aladdin; Gary Gehr and Frank Hogan at Chicago Litho; Peter Bryant, Jack Hamilton, Dave Ishman, Don Livingston, Al Mauer, Mary P. O'Neill, Charles Seltz, and Dave Taylor at King Seeley Thermos; Mike Clark, Pat Grandy, and Herb Plassmann at Ohio Art; and, Sam Costanzo and Harry S. Kammerer at Pittsburg Metal Lithography.

I wish to extend my gratitude further to those who provided parts of the puzzle; Hal Morgan and Kerrie Tucker gave me a publishing primer; Michael Haubrick opened doors in Hollywood; William M. Gaines eulogized the late Wally Wood; Larry Kent, Art Rush, and Francie Williams clarified Roy Rogers' box connection; Dale Ames and Alan Cohen put me on to Frankie Thomas; Jeff Banks, Heilda Joy, Hugo Tocchet, and Scotto Westphal scoured memories and files for leads to the mysterious Mr. Wexler; Arlene Palmer loaned rare Universal catalogs; and Peter Fritz suggested the rarity scale.

Special thanks to Dan Soper for his superb photographs, and the dedicated collectors, without whose box and bottle loans, the look of book would have been compromised: Alan and Paula Bress, Bob Carr, Lee Garner, Mark Gunter, Larry Jordan, Deb MacAndrew, Marguerite Riegel, Dave Russell, Roy Shoff, Neil St. Clair, Ray Van Jones, and Jonathon White.

Also contributing immeasurably were Ken Beck, Lucy S. Caswell, Jim Clark, Trish Flaherty, Fred Fox, Fernando Joffroy, Jeff Judson, Bill Habbersett, Kathy Hansen, Gene Lemery, Tom Lespasio, Peter Lespasio, Jerry Mathers, Doug Pelton, Anne Reed, James S. Reyburn, Cameron Shaw, Patrick Soldano, David R. Smith, Harold N. Taylor, Pat Thibodeau, Tom Tumbusch, Paramount Pictures Corporation, Taft/Hamilton Group, Archie Comics Publications, Inc., and Paladium Entertainment Corporation.

Many thanks to Judith Dunham for her excellent job of editing the manuscript.

More information on lunch box collecting may be found in the pages of the quarterly newsletter *HOT BOXING*, P.O. Box 87, Somerville, MA 02143.